The Dinosaurs' Dinner

M. Christina Butler

ILLUSTRATED BY

VAL BIRO

MACDONALD YOUNG BOOKS

It was dinner time,

For little Kate, with love (M.C.B.)

First published in Great Britain in 1997 by
Macdonald Young Books
an imprint of Wayland Publishers Ltd
61 Western Road
Hove
East Sussex
BN3 1JD

Text © 1997 M. Christina Butler
Illustrations © 1997 Val Biro

Typeset in 20pt Plantin by
Dorchester Typesetting Group Ltd
Printed and bound in Belgium by
Proost International Book Production

British Library Cataloguing in Publication Data available

ISBN 0 7500 2242 6

and the dinosaurs were hungry.

But when they reached the lake,
there was nothing for their dinner!
"Who's eaten my trees? Was it you?"
Diplodocus shouted at Triceratops.

"Someone's stamped on my palms!
Was it you?" wailed Triceratops.
"Who's gobbled all my water lilies?"
roared Stegosaurus, glaring at them both.

As they got hungrier,
the dinosaurs shouted
and yelled, and
argued and fought,
until suddenly
Stegosaurus cried,
"Well if you didn't
eat my water lilies,
then who did?"
Triceratops was puzzled.
"And who is BIG enough
to squash my palms?"
she asked.
"And STRONG enough to
break my trees down?"
Diplodocus whispered.

They looked at each other and TREMBLED!

All night the three dinosaurs had terrible dreams, about ferocious dinosaurs with big sharp teeth.

THE BIG REXES!

The next morning they decided to find somewhere safer, away from the mountains where the Big Rexes lived.

On and on they walked, day and night . . .

. . . until they found a beautiful lake
in the forest, covered in water lilies,
a long way from the mountains.

But all at once, out of nowhere . . .

there came a TERRIBLE NOISE . . .

and a FRIGHTFUL wind . . .

The trees creaked,

and the tops fell off!

The leaves of the palm bushes flew into the air!
And with a great WHOOSH! the water lilies
were thrown out of the lake!

The three dinosaurs . . .

. . . were blown off their feet,

and rolled back into a swamp!

When the wind stopped
blowing, they heard
a deep sad voice.
"Please don't go," it said,
"I want to be friends."
Diplodocus, Triceratops
and Stegosaurus climbed
out of the swamp and
looked up.

There was a huge
dinosaur in front
of them.

"I'm a Gigantosaurus from the south," she said. "I've got a cold in my very big nose, and when I sneeze, everyone runs away!"
She sniffed loudly.
"No one will be friends with me!"

The three dinosaurs
walked round the lake
to look at her.
"Don't be sad," said
Stegosaurus. "We'll
be your friends."

"Just as long as you don't
SNEEZE at us again,"
cried Diplodocus,
"and blow us away!"
"And spoil our dinner,"
Triceratops added quickly.

Then they all laughed,

and had dinner with their new friend.

GIGANTOSAURUS

STEGOSAURUS

DIPLODOCUS

TRICERATOPS

FALKIRK COUNCIL
LIBRARY SUPPORT
FOR SCHOOLS